For Dorcas
L. J.

For Mum and Dad
T. W.

First U.S. Edition

First published in Great Britain by Magi Publications

ISBN 0-316-13341-8

Library of Congress Catalog Card Number: 94-78895

10 9 8 7 6 5 4 3 2 1

Printed in Italy

TOM'S TAIL

by
Linda Jennings

Illustrated by
Tim Warnes

LITTLE, BROWN AND COMPANY

Boston   New York   Toronto   London

Tom was the sort of piglet who was never quite satisfied. When he considered his tail, he was not pleased at all. It was a neat little tail, but it was all curly-twirly. Tom wanted it straight.

In all other ways Tom was a fine little pig.

He was a nice pale pink with dirty patches here and there where he had wallowed in mud. He slurped and snuffled in the trough with all his brothers and sisters and made the usual piggy noises. But how he wished he had a straight tail!

Sam the sheepdog had
a lovely black
plumy tail.

Hannibal the horse
had a long, swishy tail.

And Geraldine the Jersey cow had a thin, stringy tail with a little tuft on the end.

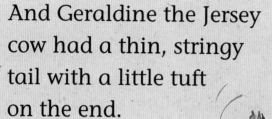

"Even the rat's tail is less curly than mine," said Tom miserably.

Very soon all the animals on Appletree Farm were fed up with Tom's complaints.
"Why don't you get your tail straightened?" said Hannibal.
"How?" asked Tom.
"Like this," said Hannibal, and he put his big hoof on the edge of Tom's tail.
"Now walk away," he said.

Tom squealed and squeaked
with the pain of Hannibal's
heavy hoof. But then, as he
began to walk . . .

. . . his tail stretched out,
and, when it had uncurled to
the very end, Hannibal let go.

PING!

Back sprang the tail . . .

. . . and Tom hurtled forward.

"OUCH!" yelled Tom and
Sam the sheepdog together.

"Tell you what," said Sam, picking himself up.
"Why don't I take hold of your tail, and you can lead
me along. That should straighten it."
So Tom took Sam for a walk, past the pigstyes . . .

. . . around the pond . . .

. . . and over the buttercup meadows. Very soon Tom's tail ached and ached.
"Let go!" he cried.

PING!
Back sprang the tail to its usual curly-twirly self.
Tom felt miserable.

Geraldine the Jersey cow
looked at Tom and chewed
thoughtfully.
Suddenly she had a
VERY GOOD IDEA.
She told it
to Sam . . .

. . . who took hold of Tom's tail again and stretched it.
It hurt terribly.
Then he pushed the tail into a big patch of gooey,
squelchy mud!

He made Tom lie with his tail covered
in mud for a very long
long time, until . . .

. . . the mud dried and Tom's tail was set into a long, thin pencil.

"YIPPEE!" cried Tom.

He twirled around, trying to see his new, straight tail.
"OUCH!" said Sam.
Tom had poked him right in the chest!

"You look very silly," said Tom's mother.
But Tom didn't care. He liked to be different.
"I'll try to wag my tail like Sam does," he said.
WHACK! The tail hit Tom's sister in the face and then
stuck his brother in the bottom.
"STOP THAT!" cried Tom's mother.

When it was dark, Tom's mother
gathered in all her piglets for
the night. They liked to
snuggle up in a big
piggy heap.
But Tom's tail got
in the way.

"GO AWAY!" cried all his brothers and sisters, and they chased Tom right out of the sty.

Poor Tom! He tried to curl up against the farmyard wall,
but it wasn't very comfortable to lie down with a tail
as stiff as a pencil.
At long last, though, he fell asleep.

In the night it began to rain, but Tom tried to sleep as best he could.

As it rained, the hard mud softened and slid off his tail.

By the time morning came, his tail was as curly-twirly as it had ever been. Grunting happily, Tom went back to the sty.

"Who wants a straight tail, anyway," said Tom later, as he pushed and shoved into the trough with all his brothers and sisters.

"However, if I could only have a long, elegant nose like Hannibal the horse instead of this silly snout, I could *really* get at the food!"